For Luke,

Jeremy
And
The
General

by
Sharon
Elwell

Sharon Elwell
11/6/14

Published by:
Rattle OK Publications
PO Box 902075
Palmdale CA 93590-2075

Jeremyandwappo@cs.com

ISBN 1-883965-45-4

PRINTED IN THE UNITED STATES OF AMERICA

Library of Congress

Cataloging in Publication Number

This book is available at discount pricing for Classroom sets of 15, 20, or 30. For information, contact the publisher.

Acknowledgements:

Many thanks to Carol Dodge, curator of the Sonoma garrison, Ben Chamberlain and Jobey Maher, editors and advisors, and Jane Forbes, who makes sure we all get the work done.

Chapter One
General Vallejo
and the 21st Century

Jeremy was sitting alone in a deserted used car lot on Redwood Road in Vallejo, California, under a huge redwood statue of General Mariano Guadalupe Vallejo, the *Californio* for whom the town was named sometime during the 19th century. The sun was going down over the north end of San Francisco Bay. In a few minutes, Jeremy would not only be alone; he would be cold.

It's possible that Jeremy was also a little bit afraid. He had followed his older brother, Salvador, about half an hour ago when Sal had left the house with his friends. Jeremy worried about his older brother. Sal and his buddies dressed like gang members. They were always laughing at jokes nobody else could understand. Salvador was grumpy to their mother, often getting into trouble for rude things he said. Things weren't looking too good to Jeremy.

When Sal wasn't around, Jeremy peeked into his older brother's backpack and dresser drawers. He also listened to his telephone conversations. He watched Sal's eyes to see if they had dilated pupils. Was he taking drugs? Was he carrying weapons? Were Sal and his friends part of a gang?

So far, Jeremy had not found any clues, but he was still worried. When two of Sal's friends had come by tonight, they had cans of spray paint in their jacket pockets. All of them were laughing. Jeremy had grabbed a jacket and followed as soon as they were out the door. A brother has a lot of responsibility, he told himself.

But the older boys walked much faster. In fifteen minutes he had lost them. Worse, now Jeremy was lost!

He sat down under the statue to think. Maybe he fell asleep as he huddled against the breeze. Maybe he was wide awake. Suddenly, he heard a deep and hollow-sounding woody voice over his head.

✳✳✳✳

"Hey, homey! What's goin' on, man? Wassup, bro?"

3

Jeremy jumped up, but there was no one nearby. The huge voice began again, "Yo! Boy in the strange clothing! You deaf?"

Jeremy was definitely afraid now. "Who's there?"

"Look up, man. It's me!"

Jeremy's eyes moved slowly up the statue. He saw that the stern face was smiling.

Jeremy looked all around. He did not want anyone walking by to see that he was about to talk out loud to a wooden statue.

"Excuse me, Mr. Statue, sir, but did you just talk? I mean, did you say something?"

"Right on, son. All right, and right back at you! We have contact!"

Jeremy shook his head. "What does all that mean? Are you trying to say something?"

The woody voice got louder. "Mean? Mean!! Don't ask me! I don't know. Doesn't it mean anything to you? It's your century! This is how you people talk. Get with the program! Get a life! Wake up and smell the orange juice!"

Jeremy had to laugh. "Coffee. Or roses or something. Not orange juice."

The statue frowned. "I like the smell of orange juice."

Jeremy shook his head. "Of course. I do, too, but the saying is...Oh, never mind."

The statue sighed, creating a gust of wind that smelled like deep redwood forests. "Once I knew French, English, Latin, Spanish...Oh, well. I should have known the information I got on the Internet about how to talk to 21st century young people would be out of date. Language changes so fast!"

Jeremy looked up. "You got all those expressions on the Internet?"

The statue nodded sadly. "In chat rooms like, 'For Kids Only'. I'm all lurking, getting the 411. I wanted to sound all like, you know, totally cold so that you could, you know, like totally understand me and we could like do some male bonding, spend some like quality time. Does any of this make sense to you? Do you like understand anything I'm like saying?"

Jeremy frowned. "Well, kind of. But how did you get on the Internet? You're a statue."

The statue laughed. "Nobody knows who you are in cyberspace, Jeremy. Generalissimo@afterlife.com. That's me! Nobody can tell if you're alive or not."

Jeremy was amazed. "You said my name! You know my name? You knew about me?"

The giant wooden head nodded with a creaking sound. "That's why I came. I know about your teacher."

"What?"

"And I know about your brother. I know the things that you're worrying about."

Suddenly Jeremy felt dizzy. He was talking to a statue – and a statue who knew a lot about him. He had felt bad when he sat down, but now he felt definitely worse!

Chapter Two
Problems Past and Present

Jeremy and General Vallejo looked at each other. "Mr. General, sir, I understand that you are... I mean, very big and important, and ..."

The statue laughed. "Well, I'm definitely big! Far too big for the city offices downtown, where I was supposed to be. This statue belongs at city hall, they tell me, but I couldn't fit. So here I am watching people buy cars. By the way, that's a great deal on this little truck right here."

Jeremy looked around at the car lot. "I know how you feel. I didn't plan to come here, either."

The statue smiled. "But here we are, my boy. And we finally have a chance to meet!"

Jeremy was surprised. "Finally? But I didn't know about you... I wasn't..."

"You haven't been waiting for a chance to meet me?"

"Well, how could I be, sir? I mean, you're dead."

The general frowned. "I keep forgetting about that! Well, that's all right. I've been waiting for a chance to meet you. You have very important work to do. The dream of California must be kept alive."

"California? I don't have a dream about California. California is just fine!"

"Ah, yes. I thought the same thing. California as I knew it was the perfect combination: the strong native peoples, the gracious good manners of the Spanish – my people – and the progressive inventions of the Yankees. Paradise! But those groups kept fighting all the way the way through my century.

"And now, in your century, there is still fighting. The Alta California Mexicans, the *Norteños*, whom we called *Arribeños*, are still fighting with the *Sureños*, whom we called *Bajeños*. And all of them are still fighting with *Norteamericanos*.

"That's a little bit disappointing, Jeremy..."

"And confusing!" said Jeremy.

11

"That, too! But I'm depending on you to improve the situation in your century: the 21st, the New Millenium!"

Jeremy's mouth fell open. "Me! What do I have to do with it?"

"You're a Californio, and we dream big dreams."

Jeremy frowned. "I'm a kid. You were different. This whole town was named for you."

"Vallejo was not my choice, young man. When I owned this property as part of my Soscol Rancho, I hoped it would become the state capital. *Eureka*! That was my name for it. Do you know what it means?"

Jeremy shook his head.

"Eureka means, 'I have found it!' Now that's a great name."

"There already is a town in California named Eureka."

"I heard about that. Up north somewhere. The redwood for this statue came from that area. Ah, well. At least somebody recognized a great name!

"In the state assembly, I also proposed a beautiful name for the state of California, but nobody liked it. Another wonderful idea wasted!" The statue sighed.

"What was it?" asked Jeremy.

"I wanted to name California after the noble Aztec chieftain, Moctezuma. How do you think that sounds? Say it a few times. Montezuma – that's how English-speaking people usually pronounce it. Would you like to be a Montezuman instead of a Californian?"

Jeremy made a face. "Don't feel bad, sir. I'm sure you had other talents."

✳✳✳✳

Jeremy and the statue were quiet for a moment, then the woody voice said, "I've been

13

standing here for several years now, and I'm a little tired. Would you mind if I sat down?"

"Of course not ...er, wait a minute!" Jeremy jumped out of the way just as the huge wooden body bent in the middle and sat down with an enormous sound like a building collapsing.

"Ah," said the general. "*¡Qué gusto*! Can you imagine what it's like to stand at attention year after year?"

Jeremy couldn't. "Can you move around?"

The general looked puzzled. "Well, let me think about that. I guess I could."

Without warning, the statue stood up again and began dancing, taking gigantic, awkward steps. Huge splinters flew in every direction.

"Yikes!" Jeremy ran behind a red Chevy Blazer.

"*¡Ay, caray*!" said the general. "That's enough of that! It's amazing how out of shape one can become with just a few decades of inactivity!" He sat back down.

❋❋❋❋

Jeremy came cautiously out from behind the cars. "What I want to know, sir, is how did you know about me?"

"Don't kids in school study the past? Don't you have history classes?"

"Well, sure, but..."

"And what do you think we who are part of the past study?"

"You don't have to study! You're grown up. You're past grown up. You're dead! You don't have to ever study again!"

The general laughed. "I hope this won't come as a disappointment, but you can't learn everything in 70 or 80 years of life. There's just too much to know!

"By the time you're my age, which is around 200 right now, you'll love to study. And part of what we study is the present, of course. We study you while you study us!"

Jeremy was shocked. "You watch our lives? That's not fair!"

The general shrugged the fringed epaulets on his wooden shoulders. "We never thought people a hundred years later would be studying us, either. It's embarrassing! We did make mistakes!"

Jeremy thought about that. "OK, but why me? I'm just a kid and you're..."

"A chunk of wood, my boy. Which of us do you think is more important to the future of California?"

"I wish you'd quit saying things like that. I don't know anything about the future of California."

"That's why I came – to help you see where you belong in history."

Jeremy laughed. "I don't belong in history. History is already over. It's all in the books!"

The general laughed out loud – a strange, hollow, sound. "History never ends, *mi hijo*. You have important things to do, but you're having some troubles, too. Salvador, and Mr. Archuleta – I mean Mr. Adams. Frankly, Jeremy, you could use a little help."

"Mr. General, I don't need...Well, maybe I am having a little trouble."

"A little trouble? I'd say you're having very big trouble, *mi hijo*! Very big trouble, indeed!"

✶✶✶✶

Jeremy's eyes filled with tears. "You do know! Why doesn't he like me?"

"*Ay, niñito*, I understand how you feel! I had Mr. Archuleta as a teacher. I still feel like crying

17

when I remember him, and that was more than 160 years ago!"

Jeremy couldn't stop talking, now that he had begun. "I studied so hard! No video games all week, my favorite shows...I didn't even talk on the phone. And I finally got my first A! I knew the answer to every question on that test with no problem at all. I actually knew all the answers!"

The statue smiled. "Good for you! You must have felt very proud of yourself!"

"Well, yeah, until the grades came back. Mr. Adams gave me an F, and he wrote NOT YOUR OWN WORK!! in big letters across the page. All the kids could see it."

"Did you talk to your *padres* about it?"

"What would be the use?" asked Jeremy. "My parents would believe the teacher before they'd believe me."

"Surprisingly enough, that isn't always true. My father believed me when it came to a showdown with Mr. Archuleta."

Jeremy looked up. "Your teacher flunked you?"

The general's face was grim. "No. But Mr. Archuleta hated children. And I'm afraid we all hated him right back."

Jeremy's curiosity was aroused. "Well, what happened?"

The general asked, "Would you like to see?" Jeremy nodded, and with that nod he suddenly left his own century.

Chapter Three
Taking a Stand

Jeremy and the general found themselves in a one-room school in old Monterey. It was a small, wooden room with a pot-bellied stove in the front corner. There was a window with thick, wavy glass. A fat cat curled in a sunny spot on the floor. Surprised, Jeremy wondered if animals were always allowed in the classroom. Before he could ask, a mouse skittered along the edge of the floor.

Barely opening its eyes, the cat pounced, then carried the mouse outside to start breakfast, jumping through a cat flap that was cut into the heavy front door. Jeremy sat on the wooden bench against the back wall to watch as the school day began.

Mr. Archuleta sat reading at his desk as his pupils, all boys, entered the room one at a time, hung their jackets on hooks on the back wall, and trooped to the front of the room. Each boy bent to kiss Mr. Archuleta's hand as he passed the large desk. The teacher paid no attention, not looking up in greeting as the boys went by.

As each boy arrived at his seat, he quickly took out a quill pen, dipped it in an inkwell on the desk and began writing with great concentration. Jeremy started to ask Vallejo what was going on, but stopped. He didn't dare make a sound.

"Don't worry," boomed the voice of the statue. "They can't hear you. Or see you either. All of this is long over. Think of it as a movie. But remember, this scene is coming from my memory, and I may not remember perfectly."

"Are you in there somewhere?"

"Oh, yes," nodded the general. "On this particular day I believe I would have been eleven years old. That's me in the second row, throwing a tiny piece of paper I have rolled into a hard pellet. I'm trying to hit my cousin, Juan Alvarado."

"A spitwad? You're throwing a spitwad? That's no way for a great general to behave!"

But when he looked around, the wooden Vallejo was gone. Jeremy was alone in the back of the Monterey classroom.

The last boy to kiss the teacher's hand made a face for his classmates to see. Some of the boys struggled not to laugh, but the teacher did not seem to notice. Mr. Archuleta stood up and began to speak.

"*Jóvenes*, as you know, today represents a very unusual day. The ship from *Baja México* has reached the harbor, and the documents you have copied are almost ready to send to the *Distrito Federál*. I'm sure that no other teacher's class could have done so well, and you are an excellent reflection of the instruction you have received. I am proud of you. Accordingly, when these last few pages are finished, you will be dismissed to go to the harbor and watch the ship unload."

The boys did not cheer, but they smiled silently at each other, and all bent over their work with serious attention and redoubled effort.

Soon the desks were empty, papers neatly spread out for the ink to dry, and the boys were marching in a line toward the harbor. The door to the classroom slammed shut, the small cat door flapping. Jeremy was alone in the schoolroom.

✳✳✳✳

At first, Jeremy thought the cat door moved by itself. It bumped and jumped. After a couple of bumps, the little door opened and a rooster came through, followed by a couple of hens. They flapped up onto the desks and began pecking at the papers. Some fell to the floor. An inkstand overturned. Important documents were covered with chicken tracks.

"Oh, no!" said Jeremy, who was powerless to help. "These kids will be in terrible trouble!"

Later, Mr. Archuleta returned, leading the boys into the room. His face was shocked, then furious. "Whose task was it to secure the room this morning?" Quickly referring to a list on his desk, the teacher read the name aloud: "Mariano

Guadalupe Vallejo." It sounded like a death
sentence.

✳✳✳✳

"Señor Vallejo, if you please, come to the
front of the room and remove your shirt. José
Castro, Juan Alvarado, please come with Mariano
to tie his hands and feet. Mariano, you know what
to do. Please come and lie down across the desk."

Jeremy could not believe his eyes. Señor
Archuleta took from a desk drawer a leather whip
with several strips attached to a handle. Each
leather strip had a steel barb tied to the end of it.

Jeremy gulped. "He doesn't really hit
people, does he? That's against the law! You can't
hit kids!"

There was no one to answer him.

Silently, the boy Mariano stood, but he
remained at his desk. José and Juan came to stand
at his side. No one moved. The classroom was
silent.

After a moment, Mr. Archuleta bowed his head. "Very well. Am I to understand that you refuse to accept your punishment? You will not comply with my commands?"

Mariano, José and Juan nodded solemnly.

"You understand that your actions will be reported to your father, Mariano. As *comandante general*, the decision regarding your punishment will be his."

The boys nodded again.

"Since my authority is called into question, I feel that I can no longer serve you in my capacity as your teacher, pending the *comandante*'s ruling. Until then, class is dismissed."

Jeremy looked up to see that General Vallejo was once again beside him on the bench at the back of the room. "What happened next?"

Chapter Four
Vallejo Remembers

"Well, we had to copy all those ruined documents all over again. And they had to be perfect, with no blots or smudges. And it all had to be finished before the ship was ready to sail, so we had a lot to do and very little time in which to do it."

"But what about the beating? Were you beaten?"

"No. Once my father learned of the situation, there were no more beatings at our school. And the governor himself came to speak to Juan and José and me. He said – and I can tell you exactly what he said because it was so important to me – he said:

> Who knows but that someday, José, Juan, Mariano, who knows but that someday the three of you may be called on to guide the destiny of our beloved province.

I never forgot it. After that, he invited us to come to his offices from time to time and he taught us personally many things he thought were important for us to understand.

"Of course, I never forgot what that cat-o-nine-tails felt like, either. That was my last time to be called upon to take a beating, but it had not been the first.

"When I became a man, I helped pass a law that made it impossible for the mission *padres* to flog *los indios,* or to take their children away from them."

Jeremy was surprised. "Wait! Your teacher beat you? The mission fathers beat the Indians? Priests beat people? Teachers beat people?"

"In those days, son, it was common for parents, teachers, and priests to use force to control others. Most boys in Mr. Archuleta's class, for example, carried scars from that whip to their graves."

"The mission fathers were cruel?"

"No, Jeremy, they were not. They came to this wild land to teach the native Americans three things: farming, horsemanship, and Christianity – all things they considered vital to a good life.

"The fathers kept nothing for themselves, but held the church's land in trust for the natives so that it would belong to them when they became skillful enough to farm it. But their methods looked like slavery to many.

"It saddens me to know that Father Junipero Serra and others whose names I esteemed from my boyhood are not honored in today's world. My father came to California as a soldier with Father Serra.

"At one point, the California senate had to decide whose statue should represent California in the capitol building in Washington, D.C.

"A majority of people thought that I – humble and simple as I was – would be the correct choice to represent California in Washington. Of course I hoped the idea would die quietly, modest as I am. Still, there was a great demand for me, and I would never wish to overrule the voice of the people.

"But in the end, Father Serra's statue was put into that great hall, and I was happy with the choice. The fathers were good men. Today, nobody sees all the good that they intended. They had a great vision of bringing all people together under God. Not a bad idea."

Jeremy was indignant. "Well, things look different now. Good people don't beat other people! Good people don't force others to do things their way! How can anybody call that good?"

"Things really do look different now, son. Very different! I guess the best comparison I can give you is a word from your century: babysitting. A strange word. Do you know it?"

Jeremy smirked. "Of course. I have to babysit my cousin all the time."

"OK. Let's imagine that you saw a baby crawling out onto a roadway full of these automobiles your century is so fond of. Would you politely ask him to stop and then explain to him the dangers to his limited size and ability among forces so much stronger and faster than he is?"

Jeremy frowned. "Of course not. He's just a baby. He wouldn't understand any of that! You'd have to just grab him and save him."

"Exactly. The mission fathers saw the indigenous people as childlike because they didn't speak or live in European ways. Indians looked to them like baby people, needing education to become civilized. They had to take them under control and 'save' them.

"In the 20th century, many people understood that native cultures were not childlike, just different. But few understood that in my day.

"I myself performed some small service in this regard, collecting a book for children about native dress and customs.

"My darling wife, Francisca, was another who had respect for native peoples. She learned the various native languages, and spoke to all of our servants in their own speech. We had as many as 600 servants at a time, so it was a huge task, but Francisca ...my Francisca! That's another story, too."

The general sighed deeply and became quiet.

The two sat together in the growing darkness, silently agreeing that the world was a strange and complicated place.

Chapter Five
More Precious than Gold

When Jeremy looked up, the scene before his eyes had changed. He and the general were on a hill overlooking a beautiful harbor, where a single ship stood at anchor.

"You see that ship, Jeremy?" The general's voice was excited. "That ship carries the most valuable cargo in the world. What do you think it is?"

"Gold? Is that ship full of gold?"

The general smiled. "No indeed, my boy. The contents of that ship are much more valuable than gold."

"What could be more valuable than gold? Diamonds? Plutonium?"

"No, Jeremy. That ship is full of books. And they came all the way from Spain."

Jeremy was disappointed. "Books? Books aren't valuable. Books are free. Anybody can get all the books they want. Just go to the library!"

"My boy, you keep forgetting. That was then. This is now. Or that was now. No, that will be then. This is then...or now...anyway, what I'm trying to remind you of, in case you've failed to notice, is that the 19th century was not always like the 21st!"

Jeremy couldn't help smiling. "I have noticed that."

"Books were very hard to get, and few people in my time could read. I was a young man when this ship came in, and I paid a lot of money to buy the whole cargo of books. But it definitely got me into trouble!"

Jeremy laughed. "How could you get in trouble for buying books?"

"I imagine that you're going to be surprised, young man. Sit down and I'll tell you about it."

And so the two sat together on the grassy hillside above the harbor and the general began his explanation.

"In the 19th Century, it was sometimes considered to be dangerous for the general public to have too much information."

"What? Information was kept secret? Why?"

"Oh, too many ideas could confuse the ignorant, make them less trusting in their leaders – that kind of thing."

Jeremy was amazed. "You weren't allowed to read?"

"Oh, we were allowed to read, but only what was chosen for us."

"By who?"

"Whom, Jeremy. By whom?"

"You don't know? You never found out?"

"Of course I found out. I was trying to tell you that your grammar is...Never mind." The general shook his head. "Anyway, it was the church fathers."

Jeremy couldn't believe what he was hearing. "But that can't be right! Churches are always trying to get people to read: literacy classes, Bible school, catechism...all churches try to help people learn to read."

"Don't forget! That was then..."

"I know, I know. But how could things be so completely opposite?"

The general had no answer. He picked up the thread of his story again. "Anyway, the books were much more important to me than the consequences. There was much to learn! I was a young man and I needed all the information I could get, and books were my source of knowledge. José and Juan agreed with me that as *gente de razón*, we needed education.

"But their girlfriends found out what we had done. They told the priest, and he demanded that I burn the books or face excommunication."

"What's that?"

"It means to be cut off from the church and all of your friends who belong to the church."

"Man! What did you do?"

"Well, I didn't burn the books. I needed an education, and I was determined to get it."

"So you were excommunerated?"

41

"Excommunicated. No. Once again, fate intervened. Or maybe God himself, who knew that my intentions were not evil. Do you want to see?"

Jeremy jumped up. "Yes! Show me what happened."

Immediately, Jeremy found himself in a room paneled with dark wood. A heavy, imposing man in priestly robes stood behind a huge desk. Three young men Jeremy recognized as José Castro, Juan Alvarado, and Mariano Vallejo stood facing the priest. They were older and taller now, but their faces looked just as grim and fearful as the day they had faced Mr. Archuleta.

"You young men understand the nature of the excommunication process. Are there any final questions?"

Juan Alvarado nodded. "Yes, Father. Is it true that the church is unable to receive donations of money from excommunicants?"

The priest looked up sharply. "Donations of money?"

"Yes. It has been my understanding that the church cannot accept money from those who have been cut off."

The priest frowned. "Well, that is true, but..."

Mariano frowned also. "It's a great pity, then, for his family was preparing a large donation to build the new wing for the *sanctorum*."

The three young men nodded, unsmiling.

"Ummm," murmured the priest. "A difficult problem! The church is ever in need of support in these lean times, when we have so many *indios* to nurture and teach."

"A shame!" muttered José.

"A terrible shame," agreed Juan, "but there's no help for it!"

"Father, we thank you for your time and effort on our behalf," said Mariano, turning to leave.

"Wait!" said the priest. "There must be a way to settle this matter to our mutual benefit. Mariano, do you absolutely agree never again to purchase a shipload of books?

"Juan and José, do you absolutely agree never again to help him in such an enterprise?"

Mariano frowned in thought, but Juan and José nodded their heads in agreement, and the priest ignored Mariano's failure to participate.

"Very well, then. On behalf of the church, we accept this contrition."

The three young men smiled. Once again, they had found a peaceful way.

❋❋❋❋

Back on the hill, Jeremy had a question. "I'm missing something here, General, sir. What was in all those books that was so important?"

"I could see that there were only three ways to make a living in California in those days: the army and cattle, politics and cattle, or just cattle. I wanted to learn about those things, and I knew I would need to understand four other subjects very well."

Jeremy was curious. "What were the four subjects?"

"One was military techniques. There was the strong possibility of continuing warfare with the native peoples, and with the Americans."

"How do you study about war?"

"Well, people write books about it, you know. Many of the great generals of history kept very careful records of everything they did.

"I studied Napoleon, and even the great Roman generals. I studied how to place weaponry and men: high ground, low ground, more soldiers here, predicting where the enemy will strike next.

It's a science, and the Romans were very good at it.

"I used that knowledge when I came up against the renegade Indian Estanislao and some of the other enemies I had to face. Thanks to the books on that ship, I knew a lot of strategies."

"What was the second thing you studied?"

"I needed to find out about statesmanship."

"You were going to have ships?"

The general laughed. "Statesmanship is not a kind of ship. Statesmanship means using power others have given you when they elect you to preside over them. How to do things for the good of all: that's statesmanship."

"I don't think they teach that any more."

"I studied the lives and teachings of great men in American history, especially George Washington, a military man like myself.

"Many times his countrymen begged him to be king. He had a lot of power over others because he was a great general and because people liked him so much. But he refused to use that power to advance his own interests. He was a statesman. He cared more for the idea of democratic government than he cared for himself."

Jeremy wondered, "So if you had been asked to be king, you would've said no?"

Vallejo looked startled. "Well, that would be a hard decision, wouldn't it? Washington deserves to be on all those quarters and dollar bills. He was a very great man. Of course, I always thought that if California ever produced its own money, I would be a logical choice for...well, you know."

"I think you'd look great on a dollar bill. Really. The whiskers on the sides are really good."

"I shaved them off, you know. When California became a state I wanted to be a modern American man. I shaved off the side whiskers and I burned all the Mexican uniforms in the town square. We were starting a new life. My beautiful uniform with the gold epaulets and the red sash…"

"General, you said there were four things you needed to know, but you've only mentioned war and statesmanship. What else?"

"Oh, yes. The other two things were diplomacy – which means dealing with people in kind ways, learning how to work together – and geography."

"Geography? You weren't an explorer."

"No, but I needed to know how to carry out military campaigns against California's enemies, and also I needed to make maps to develop my own *rancho*. So now you understand why I needed the books. I had to get an education in statesmanship, military strategy, geography, and diplomacy."

Chapter Six
Learning about Learning

Jeremy was thoughtful. "We don't do it that way now."

"What do you mean?"

"A person can't decide what he wants to learn. We all do the same things: reading, then math, then social studies, spelling, science, PE, and so on."

The general was amazed. "You can't study what you want to know? What's stopping you? You have libraries, computers, all the books you could possibly want. There's nothing that isn't available to you!"

Jeremy frowned. "You make it sound so easy!"

"Well, isn't it? Can't you just get a book, or turn on the Discovery Channel and learn whatever you want to know?"

"Yeah, but I don't...well, I mean, I never thought about choosing what to learn about."

"It's not too late! You can think about it. You're still a young man. What do you want to know?"

The general sat with his splintery chin on his hand and waited for an answer.

Jeremy was surprised to realize that he knew exactly what he wanted to learn. "I want to know about space and rockets – and time travel, since it seems to happen to me all the time – and

I'd like to know how to get really tall, like basketball players.

"I'd like to know how to get rich, and how to get a teacher fired, and ..."

The general laughed. "It sounds to me as if there are many, many things you want to know."

Jeremy was amazed. "Well, yeah. I guess I do!"

"Don't let anyone put limits on what you learn, Jeremy. It's your life. You have important work to do. I did, too. Forgive me if I sound boastful, but California couldn't have gotten along without me, and I knew it!"

"A whole state couldn't get along without you? No offense, General, but isn't that a little bit conceited?"

"You're a very important person too, son. You just don't know it yet."

"And you knew all these things when you were a kid? I saw you throwing spitwads."

"Well, I did play, of course. But I knew I was in a position to serve my people. All of us, as *gente de razón*, educated people, landowners, had responsibilities to the larger society, to those who didn't have our advantages. José became a military officer, and Juan found his life in politics.

"I served in both areas. Besides *comandante general* of the army, I was a senator, served on the committee that wrote the state constitution, and mayor, and governor, well, I wasn't really, but I surely should have been, and…"

"Are you bragging?" asked Jeremy.

"Bragging! Certainly not! I'm sharing the events of my life for your instruction, young man. I can't help it if I was somewhat illustrious, can I?"

Jeremy shrugged. "I guess not."

"But I knew there had to be a way of solving problems that did not involve violence – like gang fights and wars – or using power over others like Mr. Archuleta did. I wanted to find something beyond war or even politics."

Jeremy was definitely interested now. Was there a way to deal with gangs? With unfair treatment by teachers? If there was, he wanted to know about it!

"Let me show you something."

Jeremy looked up to see before him the beautiful seaside village of Santa Barbara. They were in front of a 19th century army barracks. A line of Mexican soldiers dressed in blue and red uniforms with red sashes and gold tassels around the knees stood at attention.

It was not hard to spot the young Vallejo. He sat on horseback before the lines of uniformed men, gold epaulets on his shoulders and an angry look on his face. He was shouting orders at the group. Just as suddenly, the picture disappeared, and Jeremy and the general were back in the 21st century, back in the car lot.

"What happened?" asked Jeremy. "Why did the video cut out? Why are we back here?"

"I'm sorry, Jeremy. I thought I could endure telling you a story that demonstrated foolishness on my part. But I find I cannot. It's just too painful to go through that period again.

"Let me just say that I was somewhat conceited, as you call it, somewhat arrogant. In the scene you almost saw, I arrested the town of Santa Barbara for failing to obey my orders."

"The town? You arrested a whole town? Can you do that?"

"Well, I did. But it was not a good idea. Such an action did not make anybody take orders from me more cheerfully! My soldiers just gave me more trouble until I finally learned to listen to them.

"Looking back, I can see that those mistakes were just as important to my education as a whole shipload of books. After all, I was only fifteen years old when I first became a cadet and twenty-three when I was promoted to *comandante*. I had to learn much from experience. But it's a hard way to learn! It took a long time for my men to trust me again."

Jeremy frowned. "I know just what you mean. Mr. Adams will never forget the times I slacked off. Now when I work hard, he doesn't believe me. He thinks I'm tricking him somehow."

The two sat together under the streetlights, lost in their individual thoughts. Finally, the general said, "Well, Jeremy, never is a long time. First you need to make it to the end of the school year."

Jeremy groaned. "Oh, man, don't remind me!"

Chapter Seven
Many Flags

The general had a faraway look in his wooden eyes. "As a young man, I believed that my worst problem was Russians."

"Russians? In California?"

"They really don't teach you much, do they? Yes, for a while, it looked as though we would lose our land to the Russians. They were anxious to claim California. You, my boy, could have grown up speaking Russian!"

Jeremy frowned silently, considering the idea.

"Then, for a while, it looked as though the Indian wars would destroy us. You might have grown up fighting Indians instead of studying them."

"Cool!"

The general smiled and shook his head. "War often seems cool to boys. When you're a man you'll know that fighting is never cool. And there were other terrible things – like the discovery of gold."

Jeremy was confused. "Wait! What could be terrible about gold?"

"Well, the Gold Rush made some people poor, not rich. I was one of them. By the time gold was found at Captain Sutter's mill, I was a very rich man. The Mexican government had paid me for my military service with thousands of acres of beautiful land in northern California.

"My *rancho* in Petaluma fed 20,000 people. When my cattle were gathered for the *matanza* you could not see the beginning nor the end of the giant herd from the eastern horizon to the west.

"Not to brag, but do you know Tamalpais, the mountain in Marin County?"

Jeremy nodded. "Yes. We climbed it once."

"Well, that mountain got its name from me. *Pais* means land or country, and *tamal* – well, even you must know what tamales are, don't you?"

Jeremy laughed. "You named a mountain after tamales?"

The general smiled. "Of course not. The mountain was named for an annual celebration I gave there. I invited the residents of California to a *fiesta* once a year."

"The residents of California? All of them?"

"Of course. It would be rude to leave anyone out, don't you agree? And we had wonderful times there. Bull and bear fights, races, dancing that lasted all night…But then came the rush to find gold.

"Suddenly, there were no workers. Every man wanted gold. My ships sat empty in San Francisco Bay. The sailors had gone to the gold fields. My crops went untended. Farmers had gone to the gold fields. There were no *vaqueros* to care for the cattle. They too had gone to look for gold. I lost all of my workers, hundreds of men. Suddenly I was no longer one of the richest men in California.

"But I later saw that these events were teaching me, preparing me to deal with the biggest challenge of my life: the invasion of our beloved land by thousands of illegal immigrants from the United States."

✳✳✳✳

"Wait!" Jeremy was puzzled again. "There can't be illegal immigrants from the United States. This is the United States. Illegal immigrants come from Mexico!"

"Oh, Jeremy! Your education..." The general shook his head. "Remember that when I was alive, California was part of Mexico."

"Mexico! California was Mexico?"

"Yes, indeed. There were two departments: Alta California, where you live now, and Baja California, which is still part of Mexico today. You do know about that, don't you?"

"Well, sure. I've heard of Baja California: Tijuana, car races, greyhound races, horse races, motorcycle races...I think they race a lot down there."

"Might as well. They did not get the beautiful part of California. But my hope for your education is slightly brighter because you do know <u>something</u> about it!

"At any rate, the northernmost point in Alta California was the settlement of Sonoma, where I lived. The United States was far away on the other side of the continent."

"I can't believe it. That seems so weird. How could California be another country?"

"Oh my boy, California has been part of many countries. California was part of Spain for 280 years. It's been part of the U.S. for less than 160 years.

"In my own lifetime, I was born a citizen of Spain, became a citizen of Mexico and died a citizen of the U.S. And all without leaving California! My parents were Spanish and my two youngest children were *Yanquis*. The 19th century was a most amazing time to be alive!"

Jeremy was shaking his head. "So California belonged to Mexico..."

"Well, not for long. Just 24 years. The Russian flag flew here longer than that: 29 years.

And when I was a young soldier, the Russians were the biggest threat to the autonomy of the department."

"What's autonomy?"

"They don't teach you vocabulary, either? Autonomy is your ability to make your own decisions."

Jeremy frowned. "Maybe they figure kids don't need to know that word because they don't have any."

The general had to smile. "Well, it's possible. What was I saying?"

"About the flags and Russian otology."

The general sighed in a discouraged way.

"Autonomy, Jeremy. Autonomy... Let's see. England's flag was up for 37 days.

"And California was an independent republic, the Bear Flag Republic – the worst time of all, from my point of view – during the summer of 1846, from the 14th of June to the 27th of July.

"And they actually stitched together a ridiculous attempt at a flag out of underwear or something to commemorate that nightmare! In Sonoma today, there's a statute of the Bear Flaggers, as if they were heroes!

"Worse, they put a bear on the state flag years later! I really argued against that in the state assembly. At least I wanted the bear to be lassoed by a *vaquero*. Another of my best ideas doomed to failure!"

"What's commemorate?"

"Jeremy, you might want to add vocabulary when you put together your list of things you need to learn more about."

Chapter Eight
The Russian Princess

Jeremy had studied about the Bear Flag revolt in Social Studies. A group of English-speaking Californians had ridden to Sonoma and taken possession of the city, putting up the flag of the Independent Republic of California in the square. He was curious about that day. "Were you there when it happened?"

"Yes, certainly." said the general sternly. "I was present for the Bear Flag Incident. I don't call it a revolt – although it was certainly revolting! It was the most terrible summer of my life. I don't want to talk about it, Jeremy.

"I'd rather tell you about the beautiful Russian Princess Helene. Now that was an adventure!"

"You had a Russian girlfriend?"

"Girlfriend? Helene was not a girlfriend! She was a fairy-tale princess on her honeymoon in scenic California when she was kidnapped by Native Americans. I rescued her, and her gratitude is one reason you aren't speaking Russian."

Jeremy frowned. "I don't know. Is it an interesting story? I don't want to see any honeymoon things. I don't like kissing and all that."

"No kissing. Maybe one or two hugs. One kidnapping. A tremendously powerful Indian, who was the best friend I ever had in this world. We called him Chief Solano.

"You may have heard the word Solano, since this whole county is named for him, which is more than I ever got!

"Of course, Solano was bigger than I in many ways. He was much taller – six feet seven inches, and I was only six feet, which was actually quite a bit taller than the average person in my century..."

"General, I think you're getting distracted here. Are you still mad at Chief Solano for being taller than you?"

"Certainly not! Well, maybe just a little."

"Oh, man! I need to show you the NBA lineup."

"I've seen it, my boy. But you have to remember that we'd never heard of steroids in those days. Anyway, what do you think? Princess

Helene or the gloomy, heartbreaking, boring summer they put up the Bear Flag?"

"Well, since you put it that way..."

"Wise choice, Jeremy. One glamorous, exotic Russian princess, coming right up!"

✳✳✳✳

"Wow!" said Jeremy as the elegant tents and uniformed soldiers surrounding Princess Helene rode into view. The princess and her new husband wore matching white fur robes and were mounted on matching white horses. "I see what you mean!"

The general beamed. "Yes, Princess Helene had heard about Fort Ross and all the beautiful forests, meadows, and beaches of California. She decided the place would be perfect for her honeymoon. If you know anything about Russian winters, you can understand."

"Snow?"

"Lots of snow! The princess and her consort landed at Fort Ross, then started south to what is now Solano County, named after you-know-who, and home to the Suisun tribe, Solano's men, friendly to us. She was captured by members of that tribe, who thought to please me by eliminating my enemies."

"But she's got soldiers with her. There must have been a lot of Indians!"

"A lot. And they were big, tall, mostly naked, and ferocious looking!"

"Can I see?"

"Absolutely! Here they come now."

Jeremy's mouth fell open as a band of tall, handsome Indians appeared in a line atop the surrounding hills. They looked angry.

"Wow!" he said again. "Are they going to kill the Russians?"

"Well, they're thinking about it, Jeremy. They were trying to help me fight my enemies. Now they will camp and wait for my orders."

Which is exactly what happened. The Suisun formed a circle around the princess and her company. Then each man squatted on the ground, silent as stone.

The princess got down from her horse to approach the Indians. Chief Solano stood, the only representative of the tribe worthy to speak with royalty. Jeremy, sitting on a rise above the meadow, leaned forward to hear.

"Wait a minute," said Jeremy. "I hear them, but I can't understand what they're saying!"

"Of course not, my boy. The princess speaks Russian and the chief, well, the chief does not. They are not understanding each other any more than you are understanding either of them."

"But they're smiling. They're acting like friends."

"Well, to tell the truth, I think the princess is enchanted with Chief Solano. It's not every day a girl gets kidnapped by a handsome chieftain."

"Well, why is he acting so friendly if he plans to kill her?"

"She's winning him over, Jeremy. Remember what I said about diplomacy? You're watching diplomacy in action. He's just as impressed with her as she is with him."

"Where's her husband? Shouldn't he be trying to defend her?"

"The prince-consort is in the tent. He does not share his wife's adventurous spirit. By the time I come to save her, she will probably not need to be saved. Nevertheless, I'm riding hard right now and should come over that western hill any minute."

71

Jeremy turned in the direction the statue was pointing and sure enough, young General Vallejo, in full dress uniform, appeared at the crest of the hill with a troop of soldiers. They drew their swords and galloped toward the group.

"Wow!" said Jeremy yet again. "You guys look great!"

"A lesson there," said the general, looking at Jeremy's baggy pants and ripped-up tennis shoes. "Appearances are critical to a good first impression."

The young Vallejo dismounted at some distance from the princess and Chief Solano. He walked directly to her, bowed deeply, and kissed her hand.

"I see you did learn something from Mr. Archuleta," said Jeremy.

The statue groaned. "Oh, the youth of today are so disrespectful! You do not appreciate our customs."

"Well," said Jeremy, "you've got to admit that kissing someone's hand is pretty gross."

"Only if it's Mr. Archuleta's hand you're kissing, my boy. The princess was quite another matter!"

Jeremy was disgusted. "I can't believe you guys. People are coming to steal your country and you're hand-kissing! You've got swords. Why did you put them away? Why don't you fight for your country?"

"Watch and see, young man, watch and see. There are many ways to defend one's country!

"In fact, fighting may always be the weakest and most desperate way to get what you need. It is to be used only when all other means of communication fail."

Jeremy shook his head. "Well, it looks to me like you're all communicating just fine. It looks more like a party than a war!"

"It felt like a party, too, my boy! I'll tune it so that you can understand what our beautiful princess is saying."

The princess was clapping her hands. "I thought my wedding was the most wonderful day of my life. But today is even better! First to be kidnapped by this handsome, godlike Indian man..."

"Oh, brother," said Jeremy. "You said it wouldn't be gross!"

The general smiled.

The princess continued, "...and then to be rescued by this equally handsome..."

"Did you hear that?" asked the general. "She thought I was equally handsome!"

"It's the uniform, General," said Jeremy.

74

The princess went on, "...equally handsome group of men in their splendid uniforms..."

"See?" said Jeremy. "I told you!"

The princess said, "...makes this the most wonderful adventure of my life. Everything I heard about California was true, General. You are living in paradise!"

Smiling silently, young Vallejo bowed again.

Jeremy looked at Vallejo with a question in his eyes. "Well? It's time! Did you tell her that California belongs to the people who live here? Did you tell her to send her people home to Russia? Did you tell her..."

"Tell her? She is a princess. One does not tell her anything unless she asks. Jeremy, even ordinary people do not always listen well to what they are told."

Jeremy looked at the ground. "You mean me, don't you?"

The general smiled. "Well, as they say, if the boot fits, you must wear it!"

"Shoe!" said Jeremy.

"Shoe?"

"That's the saying: if the shoe fits, wear it!"

"Oh," said the general. "Well, as I was trying to say, people don't always listen to what they're told. But they always listen to what they say themselves. Now listen to what the beautiful Helene will say next. I had no need to say a word! "

The princess said, "General, I see that this country properly belongs to you and to the wonderful native friends who support and defend you. I have no deeper wish than that you may enjoy it forever. When I return to Russia, it is my intention to have papers drawn ceding all of

Russia's interest in California. We will leave you in peace."

Again, the general bowed deeply. "My dear princess, I am overwhelmed. And most humbly grateful!"

The princess curtsied in return.

Jeremy rolled his eyes. "There's an awful lot of bowing in your century!" he said.

"I know," smiled the general. "Fun, isn't it? Well, young man, there's nothing more to watch here. Just the campfire, the shared dinner, the wine, the dancing, the storytelling, and the peaceful night under the stars."

"Boring!" said Jeremy.

The general was suddenly stern. "It was not, my boy. War was avoided. Peace was restored. Lives were saved. And California was left safely in the hands of the Californians – all without any act of violence. Isn't that amazing?

"And even though I wasn't killing anyone in a war, I got to wear that magnificent uniform. I was a general who didn't have to fight: the best of both worlds!"

Jeremy had to smile.

Chapter Nine
The Incident

"You were right," said Jeremy. "I'm glad I saw that one about the princess."

"I'm pleased! Because you may not feel as good about the next one. It was hard, but we can't really pretend it didn't happen. Although I would like to."

"You're talking about the Bear Flag Rev...er, incident, aren't you? I thought you said we weren't going to watch it!"

"I don't want to revisit that situation. But you need to understand, so we can't be controlled by my emotions.

"But be prepared! It's a boring, confusing, discouraging, and – I have to say this – stupid story!"

"Oh, great! I have to get dizzy just to watch something boring and stupid?"

The general looked surprised. "Time travel makes you dizzy? You never mentioned that!"

"I never have a chance. We just suddenly go somewhere else."

"Well, let's try a slow transition this time. Let me paint the scene for you. Picture the dawn of a glorious June day in the Valley of the Moon. Most of Sonoma is still asleep. The mission friars are preparing to go into the fields with their neophytes."

"Is that an insect?"

The general threw back his head and laughed. "No! In fact, you yourself are a neophyte. It just means people who are new at doing something, as the Indians were new to farming. Everyone is a neophyte in some area."

"Even you?" asked Jeremy. "Are you a neophyte?"

General Vallejo considered. "Well, I certainly am trying for the first time to communicate with a person who's still alive on earth. That makes me a neophyte time traveler."

"I get it. Okay. Go ahead with the picture."

"Ah, yes," said the general. "A beautiful summer day: Cattle are grazing in pastures. Clouds are drifting; grasshoppers are buzzing."

"I know about that kind of day. You don't have to keep going."

"That's too bad!" said the general. "I was just getting warmed up to this picture-painting. Anyway, it's morning in early summer. The sun is rising. Life is good. Suddenly, all of that is reversed."

"It started to rain?" asked Jeremy.

"No, I'm not talking about the weather. The human atmosphere changed. Over the east hills from the Napa Valley rode the most disreputable group of men I had ever seen. Come to think of it, I haven't seen worse since, either!"

"I hate to ask another one," said Jeremy. "Please don't say anything about my vocabulary. But what's disreputable?"

"It means the kind of person nobody could respect. The kind of person whose appearance gives them a bad reputation."

"That's a great thing to call somebody! I can use that word. Disreputable. You disreputable scum-sucking, yellow-bellied slimeball! Now that's the first word we've learned that I can really use!"

"Don't make me worry about modern youth, Jeremy! Disreputable may be fun to say, but it is a very bad thing to be, and those men deserved the word. My task for that day was one of the supreme challenges of my life."

"You had to fight with them."

"No, child. Exactly the opposite. I had to keep from fighting them. Can you imagine how hard that would be? I had a temper like anyone else. Notice that I say, 'had,' because of course that's a thing of the past."

"You mean dead people never get mad?"

"I don't know about the others, but I am a person of great dignity and calm – I was even in my lifetime. Those men pushed my patience to the outer limits. But I had family and townspeople to protect. I couldn't afford to give in to anger. It was a very hard day!"

Okay," said Jeremy. "I'm interested. What happened?"

Instantly, Jeremy found himself inside the scene General Vallejo had described. The slow lead-in did not seem to help. He was definitely dizzy, and sat down on a huge boulder in the town square.

The air was warm. The dirt road was dusty. There were flowers, bees, blue sky, grass – all the scenery of a peaceful summer day that the general had described. In a few seconds, Jeremy felt better.

General Vallejo's two-story adobe was silent in the rising sun when a group of about thirty men on horseback rode into the square.

Seeing that Jeremy was listening, Vallejo began the story: "When my servant woke me, I went immediately to the window and sized up the group. They were so dirty that they were greasy. And noisy! It looked as if they had been riding – and possibly drinking – all night. Their very presence in that condition was an insult to me and to my family. There was only one thing for me to do."

"Call for your soldiers?"

The general sighed. "No. There had been forty soldiers in the Sonoma barracks, but I had recently disbanded my garrison because I couldn't pay them. The troops were gone."

"So you got out your guns?"

The general frowned. "Certainly not. I did not want my behavior to resemble these illiterate savages!"

"So you rolled out the cannon?"

"No, no – it was not a time for violence of any kind!"

Jeremy was shocked. "You ran away? You ran out the back door?"

The general was horrified. "Run away? Never in my life or after it. One can never run away from trouble. You have to stand and face it."

"So you faced them? You went out to talk to them?"

"No, I invited them into my home – as soon as I had on my best uniform, of course. That takes a few minutes"

"You put on all those tassels and the red sash and the hat and everything?"

"Remember what we learned in the last chapter, Jeremy. Appearances can be very important."

"And then what did you do?"

"I invited them in for *refrescos*."

Jeremy shook his head. "I can't believe it. You defended your castle by inviting the bad guys to come in and have refreshments?"

The general laughed. "My castle. I like that. My castle! Yes, I chose to defend my castle by inviting the bad guys, as you call them, inside."

"You were planning to poison them, right?"

"Well, something like that. I was planning to surrender."

Chapter Ten
The Surrender

Jeremy was horrified. "You just surrendered without a fight? I don't get it!"

"They didn't get it either. They didn't know – although they certainly would have if they had paid any attention to current affairs – that I was more anxious to see California become part of the United States of America than they were.

"Unfortunately, it was not their plan to join the United States, although none of us, and actually most of them, did not understand that at the time."

"Well, what were they doing, then?"

"It was their intention – at least some of them; they were not completely together in this plan – but they wanted to establish the Independent Republic of California! Have you ever heard of anything so foolish?"

Jeremy was not so sure. "Sounds kind of cool to me. California could be its own country. What's wrong with that?"

The general explained. "How could there be an independent California when every nation in the world wanted to claim this place? Who could defend it?

"But the Bear Flaggers wouldn't listen, and did establish their silly republic. It lasted, as I told you, from the 14th of June to the 27th of July, when the U.S. finally took charge. And during that time they kept me – me! Who loved America more than any of them – a prisoner in Sutter's Fort in Sacramento.

"If the American consul in San Francisco hadn't intervened on my behalf, I could've stayed there…it doesn't bear thinking about. But their silly plan came to nothing. I could have told them before they began that they were wasting everybody's time!"

"I'm confused," said Jeremy. "I thought you said you surrendered to them because you wanted to become part of the United States of America."

"That was the whole problem. When these men demanded my surrender, I asked plainly, "To whom?"

"When they indicated that they represented the U.S. I was more than willing to surrender. But unknown to me – and, as I said, to most of them – they did not in fact have any authority from the government. In fact, when a Mr.Grigsby found out that President Polk had not authorized them to accept my surrender on behalf of Mexico, he immediately quit and went home. He took all the brains in that group with him, I'm afraid. You'll see what I mean. Let's watch."

✳✳✳✳

A tall man pounded on the door of the adobe, and the general himself answered, bowed deeply, and held the door open to let him in.

"General Vallejo, we've come to demand your surrender!"

"And you shall have it, gentlemen. What are your terms?"

The tall man was obviously confused. "Terms? There are no terms. We win. You lose. That's all there is to it."

The general's face was stern. "Well, what exactly do you intend to take from us? Our lives? Our homes? Our land? Our herds?"

The men were deeply offended. "Certainly not!"

The general spoke patiently. "Would you object to a written record of that statement so that I can assure my fellow Mexicans that they are perfectly safe?"

The men looked at one another. The tall man was first to speak. "Well, no. I guess not."

"Thank you, gentlemen. You are most kind. Permit me to offer you some refreshment. As you know, our Sonoma wine is of excellent quality. I'll bring you pen and ink."

Outside the adobe, Jeremy watched through the window as the group of men seated themselves around a large table. Almost immediately, one of them fell asleep with his head on the table.

"Have you already surrendered?"

"Yes. At this point, they're trying to write up the terms of surrender."

"Why is that man asleep?"

"That man, Jeremy, is the famous – or infamous – Ezekiel Merritt. The others are Grigsby, Semple and Knight. In accepting my hospitality, they all overdid themselves a little bit, especially friend Merritt there."

"What happened?"

"I'm trying to tell you that Zeke Merritt has had too much to drink. He attempted to write the terms of surrender I requested from him, but he couldn't think of any. 'We won. You lost. That's all there is to it. There are no terms!' That's what he said.

"I asked for a written record of the agreement, and now hours have passed as they try to produce one. See that scratched-out piece of parchment on the table, and the others on the floor? In the meantime, the men out here are getting more and more upset."

Jeremy looked behind him at the group sitting in the square. They were disputing angrily among themselves, passing wine that the general's servants had brought to them. Finally, one man broke from the group and stormed up to the adobe, pounding on the door.

"What's going on in there? We've been out here in the hot sun for hours! The men are drinking, and it's getting harder to control..."

Just then a grinning man opened the door. "Hello, Ide. Have some wine?"

"Grigsby! You're drunk!"

Grigsby frowned. "Certainly not! We've just been enjoying...did you know the general makes some of the finest wine in California? Maybe the world! It's delightful!"

93

"Delightful? Delightful! We're at war! You're on a mission! What are you thinking of?"

Grigsby frowned again. "Me? I'm thinking of my country, the United States of America, which these fine people will soon share with us." He struggled to his feet and began to sing, "Be it ever so humble, there's no place..."

Ide lost all patience. "Share with us? These Sonoma men: Mariano Vallejo, Salvador Vallejo, Jacob Leese – they're prisoners of the Independent Republic of California!"

"I wasn't finished," said Grigsby, offended. "Be it ever so humble, there's no place like home."

Ide threw his hat to the floor and stomped on it with both feet. "It's not to be tolerated! Who could tolerate such behavior? Goldang it all, anyway! Did you demand Vallejo's surrender?"

Semple raised his head from the table. "Well, of course we did, Billy. We demanded properly and he surrendered properly."

Ide was surprised. "You mean we did it? We conquered the Mexicans?"

Knight said, "Of course we did. We've just been working on the terms of surrender. That's the hard part."

Ide looked at Vallejo for the first time. "Terms? What do you mean, terms?"

Vallejo responded slowly, "Please. Have a seat, Mr. Ide."

Ide answered firmly, "No, thank you. What do you mean, terms? You Mexicans have kept us Americans from buying land or even renting it. You can't shut us out any longer!"

Vallejo nodded. "Well, I cannot compromise the safety of those who rely upon me. As part of the surrender I want it to be made clear that the lives and property of the Mexican inhabitants of Alta California will be quite safe."

Ide drew himself up to his full height. "You can rely on the honor of United States citizens, General."

Vallejo bowed. "I never doubted it, sir. But as you know, this historical transaction involves many more people than ourselves. It will be in everyone's best interest if the terms are clearly expressed in writing for all to see."

Ide folded his arms and frowned. "That's idiotic! You lost. What else is there to say?"

"That you do not intend to rob us of our property."

Ide sat down at the table. "Very well."

✳✳✳✳

Watching from outside, Jeremy questioned the statue. "Did he do it?"

"Well," said Vallejo, "he tried. He definitely tried, but these men were ill-equipped to be founding fathers of a new republic. They weren't prepared to accept a surrender. They had only prepared for a fight – and not very well. Again, hours went by."

※※※※

As Jeremy watched, Ide stood and read the surrender to the other men.

> Article 1: Vallejo is to admit himself a prisoner and agree not to take up arms against his captors.

> Article 2: In return, the safety of the families and property of these men is guaranteed. No resident of the jurisdiction is to be disturbed.

> Article 3: The representatives, having resolved to establish this new government upon republican principles, having no

regular plan of government, feel it our duty to say that we do not intend to take or injure any person not found to be in opposition to our cause, nor to take property further than is necessary for our support."

Ide was obviously proud of his work. "What do you think?"

Merritt was back asleep on the table, but the others nodded. Knight raised his hand and said, "Aye."

"Very well, then" said Ide. "I'll take this list to the men outside."

The meeting outside was amazingly brief. In a few minutes, Ide was back inside the door, breathing hard.

"It's not going to work!"

Vallejo became alert. Merritt lifted his head.

"Not work? How can it not work?"

"The men outside say they want to confiscate all the general's property and divide it up. They say they aren't going without some reward for their work: houses and gold!"

General Vallejo sat down. It was easy to see his strong feelings as he clenched and opened his fists, but he chose not to speak.

"We could send to Fremont or Captain Sutter for a determination," said Ide, muttering to himself. The others seemed too confused to speak.

Chapter Eleven
A Prisoner

At that moment, there was a knock on the door. Grigsby came back into the room. "Ide, I'm afraid there's been some misunderstanding here. The men and I need clarification."

"Yes?" said Ide.

"Do we or do we not have authority from Captain Fremont to accept Vallejo's surrender of this territory for and in behalf of the United States?"

Vallejo looked up sharply.

Ide shook his head. "We're acting as independent agents, and have the intention of establishing an independent republic."

Grigsby's mouth fell open. "Well, I'll be...I rode all this way? You're no better than a group of brigands! And I helped you! I was recruited under false pretenses of the very worst kind. I'm leaving before we get our throats cut!"

He turned to General Vallejo and bowed. "Mr. Vallejo, my most profound apologies. You will experience no further difficulty on my account."

Vallejo frowned. If this man of honor went home, the voices of reason were getting fewer. Just then, the men outside, seemingly out of patience, rushed the door. Their banging made Jeremy jump.

✳✳✳✳

Vallejo quietly opened a desk drawer and took out a gun, which he tucked into his sash and carried into a nearby drawing room. There Señora Francisca Vallejo sat beside a tiny coffin. Jeremy looked at the general questioningly, and was surprised to see tears on his cheeks.

"What is it?" Jeremy whispered to the statue beside him.

"In those days, *mi hijo*, we lost about half of the babies that were born. My Francisca has just suffered the loss of another baby. Of our sixteen children, only ten survived."

Jeremy could not understand what the general was saying. "You mean they died? Half the babies died? How could that be?"

"There were many reasons, Jeremy. Disease. We didn't have immunizations then. We didn't know about the importance of cleanliness and hygiene.

"And at this terrible moment, while all the negotiations with these fools are in progress, my dear wife's feelings are tormented by the recent loss of this baby. She sits in mourning, but I don't dare leave her undisturbed in her grief.

"Men of every kind and creed had always been welcome in our house until that very morning, but if those wild men outside came into our home, she needed to be prepared to defend herself."

"Did she know how to shoot a gun?"

The statue smiled. "My wife was an amazing woman, Jeremy. There was very little she didn't know how to do. And a good thing it was, too, because before this particular day was over, she would be called upon to manage the affairs of our household and the community for several weeks."

✳✳✳✳

Jeremy looked up. "What happens to you? Where are you going?"

The statue was silent.

"Look, General, if you don't want to talk about this, let's go back. I don't need to see these things."

The statue shook its head. "No, Jeremy. That's just the point. You do need to see them. I was taken from my grieving wife at gunpoint and tied onto a horse. Our friend Señor Prudon and my brother Salvador..."

Jeremy interrupted. "Wait! You have a brother with the same name as mine?"

"Indeed. And my Salvador had a hot-headed propensity for trouble. I chose not to believe much of what was told to me about him, but he caused me many an uneasy moment, I can tell you. During the summer of our painful Bear Flag experience, he nearly got us all killed.

"He shouted insults and threats at the North Americans while we prepared to leave. I was afraid for your lives for a few minutes, but we managed to calm him and he was taken on horseback, as I was, to spend the summer miserably imprisoned in Captain Sutter's Fort in Sacramento. Salvador didn't speak during that whole journey, but I could feel his fury. He was a proud man, and the humiliation nearly choked him.

"It didn't do me much good, either, of course, but since I am blessed with a quiet calm and deep humility, I was able to endure it better."

Jeremy didn't mean to, but he was so surprised at this statement that he laughed out loud. Then he looked up to see if he had offended his wooden friend. To his surprise, General Vallejo had also begun to laugh.

Chapter Twelve
Avoiding Rescue

" The big problem now, of course, was how not to get rescued," the general began.

"I'm sorry, sir," said Jeremy. "I thought you said how <u>not</u> to get rescued."

"I did!" said Vallejo. "If we were rescued from the Bear Flaggers, it would spoil everything! It would be much more difficult to be accepted into the United States of America if we were found to have put up a resistance to the Americans.

"But Chief Solano, of course, didn't see it that way. I finally was able to persuade him that he needed to remain in Sonoma to ensure the safety of Francisca and the children. But he was not the only would-be rescuer.

"After riding many miles that first day, we stopped at the rancho of Don Manuel Vaca, in what is today called Vacaville, to sleep for the night.

"Don Cayetano Juarez, our good friend from Napa, had received word of our situation. You can imagine my surprise when a woman walking quietly through our area turned out to be Don Cayetano's brother in disguise. There were riders waiting just outside the camp. Don Cayetano had sent them to rescue us!

109

"It took all my powers of persuasion to send him away before he got caught in that silly dress. Our captors would never have believed that we knew nothing of the plot.

"As we rode together the next day, William Semple and I became good friends – and later went into business together. And, of course, kindly Captain Sutter was…"

Jeremy shook his head. "Stop! You're confusing me, General. I'm mixing up the good guys and the bad guys! Semple had taken you prisoner and Sutter was the one who kept you in jail."

"That's right."

"So how can you say that you became good friends? Those people weren't your friends! It's almost like you couldn't tell a friend from an enemy!"

The general sighed. "All right. That's a fair question. Now I'm going to try to tell you something important. And I want you to pay attention, because we don't have much time left to visit. Your brother Salvador will be here any minute."

Jeremy realized that they were back in the car lot, alone on the asphalt. He looked around. "Sal's coming? How do you know?"

"That's one of the gifts people have who are no longer living, Jeremy. We can see much more than you can from your position."

Chapter Thirteen
Friends and Enemies

"All right," said Jeremy. "I'm listening.

"Good, my boy. Good."

"But I don't want us to stop talking. You said you'd help me know what to do about Mister Archuleta – I mean Mr. Adams – and about my brother, too. We haven't even talked about those things! Can't we visit more? Can't we talk again?"

The statue climbed back into his straight position and shook his head, straightening his lance. "I'm afraid not, my boy. But if you'll remember what you've learned tonight, it will be enough."

Jeremy heard a familiar whistle across the street. "Hey, little brother! What are you doing out here?"

"Hurry, General! He's coming! What was it you wanted to tell me?"

"I've heard young people say to one another, 'You're history!' I think they say it when they beat somebody at a game, but it's a true phrase. "You *are* history, Jeremy. The world you see around you now, the countries, the states, the cities, and even the car lots were all somebody's dream once, somebody's plan.

"The future will be whatever *you* plan for, and whatever *you* dream about. The world belongs to you now. It's your turn on earth. So remember those of us who took our turn before you.

"Study my mistakes as I studied Caesar and Napoleon. Then you won't have to make those same errors for yourself. And study, too, the things we did right. You'll have some strategies.

"I learned in my lifetime that people were not always what they seemed to be. Semple seemed to be an enemy, but he became a friend. Fremont seemed to be a friend, but he was an enemy to me and to his own people, the Americans. He was later court-martialed for his lies.

"Sutter was my jailer, but not by his own choice. We had many long conversations that taught me a great deal. You can't always judge people by appearances…I must go. Salvador is coming! Think carefully, Jeremy!"

"But you haven't told me what to do!"

"I have confidence in you, boy. That's why I chose to talk with you. Remember what you've learned tonight and you'll know what to do!"

Sal was running across the street toward Jeremy. "You shouldn't be out here all alone, little brother! What are you doing?"

Suddenly Jeremy felt like crying. "I was trying to catch up with you guys, but you went so fast, and I called you, but you didn't hear me, and…"

"Wait a minute! You've been out here all this time? Since I went to the school carnival? Why didn't you just turn around and take yourself back home?"

"Well, I was…did you say school carnival?"

"Yeah, the guys had to paint the signs for the school carnival tomorrow. If you'd asked me, I'd have taken you with us. Why don't you say something once in a while?"

Sal put his arm around Jeremy's shoulders. "Man, you're cold! Here, take my jacket. I'm too hot anyway. I've been working hard putting up those signs all night."

Jeremy couldn't help smiling. "That's what you were doing? Putting up signs at school?"

"Yeah. What did you think? I'm on the student council, man. I have to help with everything that goes on at that school. But I don't mind. It's usually pretty fun.

"Let's get home! I could use some hot chocolate, and I'm anxious to talk to Mom." The boys turned and started walking.

Jeremy was worried. "Talk to Mom? What about?"

"Oh, I lost my temper again tonight and I know I hurt her feelings. Sometimes I say things I don't mean before I can stop and think. She's probably home crying right now, thinking about what a jerk she's raising for a son!"

Jeremy nodded. "It must have something to do with your name."

"My name? Why?"

"Well, Salvador Vallejo was just like that!"

"Salvador Vallejo? Who's he?"

"General Vallejo's brother."

"General Vallejo? You mean the guy with the statue?"

"Yeah."

"How'd you find out about his brother? You doing a report or something?"

"Yeah, kind of."

"I'm glad to see you're getting your schoolwork done. How are you getting along with your teacher?"

"Mr. Adams? He's terrible! But I can handle it."

"Where'd that come from?"

"Well, you can never run from trouble. You have to stand and face it. You know what I mean?"

"You're going to talk to him?"

"Yes." Jeremy was surprised to hear himself say that. He hadn't known until that very minute that he planned to make an appointment and talk to Mr. Adams. But now that he said it, it sounded just right. "I've got plans for my life, you know, and I have to be in charge of my own education."

Salvador stopped walking. "Excuse me?"

Jeremy stopped, too. "What?"

"I thought you said you had to be in charge of your own education. I thought you said you had plans for your life."

"That's right."

"Are you sure you're old enough to be thinking about such grownup stuff?"

Jeremy pulled himself taller inside Sal's jacket. "Some people think so."